The Boxcar Children Mysteries

THE GHOST SHIP MYSTERY

created by
GERTRUDE CHANDLER WARNER

Illustrated by Charles Tang

SCHOLASTIC INC.
New York Toronto London Auckland Sydney

ISBN 0-590-46938-X

12 11 10 9 8 7 6 5 4 3 2 1   4 5 6 7 8 9/9

Printed in the U.S.A.

First Scholastic printing, February 1994

Contents

CHAPTER 1

All Aboard!

Four shivering children stood next to a big black stove. They were all wrapped up in white towels.

"I think my hat blew a-w-w-w-a-y," six-year-old Benny Alden said through chattering teeth. "I hope it didn't land in the ocean!"

James Alden, the children's grandfather, gave Benny a hug. "Not to worry, Benny. Mr. Pease got all our things from the car nice and dry. See?"

Just then, a man with a jolly face stepped into the kitchen of the Black Dog Inn. He was carrying several suitcases and wearing a bright yellow rain slicker. On his head was Benny's missing sailor cap. "All hands on deck!" the man said with a smile.

Benny grinned and saluted. "That's my hat on your head," he told the man.

Everyone laughed. "Mr. Pease, these are my grandchildren," James Alden said. "The boy who belongs to that sailor cap is the youngest, Benny. And those three shivering children are Violet, Jessie, and Henry. You'll be able to tell them apart when they're not all dressed up in towels. Mrs. Pease thought they might like to dry themselves in your warm kitchen. Why, that wind and rain just soaked through us in no time at all."

"Indeed!" Mr. Pease said. "That's a gale blowing up. Yessir. First one of the season. Ragged Cove is about to be hit by a storm. A big one, too. You folks are in for an adventure."

"Adventures are what we like!" announced Henry, who was fourteen.

"Your grandfather told me you'd say that!" Mr. Pease said. He put the sailor cap on

Benny's head. "And he said nobody's better in an emergency than his grandchildren. I don't know if you mind being guests who help instead of guests who get help. With this storm coming up so fast, I could use a few extra hands."

"I'm a good worker," Benny said.

"And a good eater," Mrs. Pease added as she came into the big cheery kitchen. "Benny has already eaten one of the johnnycakes I finished frying up on the griddle. I'll have to start calling them Bennycakes. How about another one, Benny?"

"Yum," Benny said.

"First I'll take you up to your room so you can put on some dry clothes," Mrs. Pease said. She led the children up the creaky stairs of the old whaling captain's house that was now an inn. The Aldens were staying there while Mr. Alden did business in the old seaport town of Ragged Cove, Massachusetts.

"I had to send the staff home early because of the storm," Mrs. Pease told the children. "I'm so glad you don't mind pitching in."

"We can be your junior staff," twelve-year-old Jessie said. "We like to help out."

"Mr. Pease and I are glad to have some young people at the Black Dog. Our own grandchildren live a long way off. We don't see nearly enough of them," Mrs. Pease said. "Now here's your room. It's called the Crow's Nest. It's taller than the rest of the inn and looks out over everything, just like the crow's nest on a ship."

Mrs. Pease opened a narrow wooden door to reveal a snug room with tidy bunk beds and chests built into the walls.

"Oh, look, a little porch right outside our room!" cried ten-year-old Violet. "I can go out there to paint seascapes when the weather gets better."

"That's called a widow's walk, Violet," Mrs. Pease explained. "Back in the whaling days of Ragged Cove, the wives of sailors could stand there and watch for their husbands' ships to return."

"Then why isn't it called a wife's walk?" Benny asked.

Jessie Alden, who loved history, answered. "Well, Benny, so many of the husbands died at sea, these lookouts got to be called widows' walks."

"That's so sad," Violet said in a quiet voice.

"I bet a lot of ships were lost on days like this," Henry added.

"Quite a lot," Mrs. Pease told the children. "My mind is at ease now that Mr. Pease has retired from his fishing boat. I don't have to come up here to look out for him on these stormy days. He's a lot safer helping me run the Black Dog Inn than piloting the *Sea Dog*."

Benny finished drying his hair with his towel, and put on his sailor cap. "We have a dog Watch, but he had to stay home. He's not a sea dog, though — he's a plain old house dog. But before we came to live with Grandfather, he was a watchdog in our boxcar in the woods. We fixed up the boxcar all by ourselves after our parents died. We lived there until Grandfather found us."

Mrs. Pease helped Benny straighten out his cap so it looked like a real sailor's hat. "Well, you'll have to meet Blackie, our watchdog. You can't run an inn called the

Black Dog and not have a black dog, right?"

"Right!" the children agreed.

The Aldens changed into dry clothes in the tiny boat-sized bathroom just off their room. It felt good to put on dry shirts and pants.

Mr. Pease knocked on the door of the Crow's Nest. "I'm needing a first mate and some cabin boys and girls," he announced. "Even green hands will do!"

Benny raised both hands. "What about these? They're not green, but they're clean."

Mr. Pease laughed. "So they are. 'Green hands' are what we sailors like to call new-comers."

The Aldens lined up to hear what Mr. Pease wanted them to do.

"Now," Mr. Pease began, "I just heard on the radio that the worst of the gale is going to hit in a few hours. They'll be needing me down at the docks to secure the boats. If you mates can help my wife pull in all the shutters and deliver emergency supplies to the guests, that would make everything shipshape."

"Let's get started," Henry said.

Mr. Pease showed the children how to pull in the shutters. The Aldens went around to all the windows and did the same. Henry was about to pull down the last latch when Benny said, "Hey, look out that way!" He pointed toward the ocean. "There are lights flashing over there."

The other children raced to the window and looked out. Sure enough, they could see wavy fingers of light shining on and off in the distance.

"What are those lights, Mr. Pease?" Henry asked. "A lighthouse? It couldn't be a fire since it's raining so hard."

Mr. Pease seemed to know right away what the boys were talking about. "Well, it might be lightning. But some folks around here believe those are the lights from a ghost ship, the *Flying Cloud*. Sank in 1869, less than a mile from here, out by Howling Cliffs. Yessir, that's what folks believe."

For once Benny Alden didn't have anything to say. His mouth formed a little circle of surprise, but no words came out.

Violet couldn't take her eyes off the swirl-

ing lights. "A gh — ghost ship?" she said in a small voice.

"Now, now, it's probably just lightning," Mr. Pease told Violet when he saw how scared she looked. "The only time we see the lights is when there's a big storm like this. Probably just our mixed-up weather. Who knows?"

Violet clicked down the shutter latch. She didn't want to see those strange lights anymore. The room was dim now.

"Your grandfather told me you children always have flashlights handy," Mr. Pease said. "Well, bring 'em along. Never know when the power might go out in a gale like this."

Benny liked this thought almost as much as the idea of a ghost ship. He found his nice yellow flashlight and stuck it in his pocket.

There were twelve guest rooms in the Black Dog Inn, so the Aldens were very busy for the next few hours. They delivered emergency flashlights and bottled water to every room and helped Grandfather build a roaring fire in the sitting room downstairs.

Soon the storm was howling against the building.

"It's nice to be inside on a day like this," Mr. Alden said. He looked around the cozy sitting room. The Black Dog Inn was snug as could be.

Also snug as could be was Blackie, the Peases' black Labrador. He thumped his tail a few times when the Aldens patted him. Then he went right back to his afternoon nap by the fireplace.

"Blackie spent the last couple of hours with Mr. Pease down at the docks," Mrs. Pease explained. "Everybody with a boat is bringing it in or anchoring it extra tight. The poor dog is tired from all the excitement."

"We're not!" Benny said. "We're having fun!"

"That's good," said Mrs. Pease. "I'm getting all my evening cooking underway now, in case the electricity goes out later. Why don't you children relax and curl up by the fire like Blackie?"

Now curling up by a fire wasn't Benny Alden's idea of excitement. Instead he followed Mrs. Pease into the kitchen.

"May I help make something?" Benny asked. "Mrs. McGregor, our housekeeper, likes us to help her cook."

"I certainly like a good helper myself," Mrs. Pease said. She handed Benny a long wooden spoon. "You can stir this cornmeal batter until you don't see any dry spots."

Benny boosted himself up on a stool and stood over a big bowl of yellow batter. He stirred and stirred. "What is this anyway?" he asked Mrs. Pease.

"Cornmeal batter for Bennycakes!" she answered with a laugh. "At breakfast we have them with sausages and maple syrup. At teatime, we eat them with jam or good, sweet butter. The Black Dog Inn is famous for them."

When the other children came into the kitchen to check on Benny they found him watching Mrs. Pease drop spoonfuls of the yellow batter onto a sizzling griddle on the big black stove.

"Violet and I can flip them," Jessie said. "Henry and Grandfather are outside tying down the lawn and porch furniture."

Soon, the three Aldens had a golden pile of warm cakes stacked and ready to take out to the sitting room. The guests had just gathered around the tea table when a huge gust of wind rattled the windows and shutters. The lights dimmed a few times, went back on, then went dark for good.

Everyone gasped, but the firelight and the Aldens' flashlights made everyone feel safe. Mrs. Pease brought in some battery-powered lights so their guests could go on reading and playing games.

Mrs. Pease opened a big wooden chest. "Here are some nice thick blankets if anyone feels chilly," she said. "We'll be losing heat soon, so anyone who wants to sleep down here should feel free. Henry Alden has volunteered to keep the fires roaring until we get power back."

"Let's get our sleeping bags," Jessie whispered to Violet. "We can snuggle by the fire with Blackie. Then it won't matter a bit that the heat is off."

A few minutes later the girls had laid out

all the sleeping bags in the sitting room.

Benny was the first one to get inside his. "It's time for stories," he announced.

"Here! Here!" several guests who were also in the sitting room agreed.

An older man held up a green book. "How about a story from this collection of sea tales? I just started to read a ghost story called 'Watery Grave: The Wreck of the *Flying Cloud.*' It's about a ship that went down right near Ragged Cove."

"Oooh," Violet and Benny said. They pulled their sleeping bags up to their chins.

The man with the book turned to Jessie. "My old eyes aren't the best in this dim light. Now young lady, I've noticed you have a nice clear voice and sharp eyes. How about reading us the tale?"

Benny looked up at Jessie with hopeful eyes. "Would you, Jessie? Please? Read us something scary."

Jessie opened the faded old book and began to read.

CHAPTER 2

A Fire at Sea

Jessie had been reading for fifteen minutes. Her throat was dry, but she couldn't stop. There were only a few pages left:

"In November 1869, there was still no sign of the Flying Cloud. *Every day for two years, Emily Coffin climbed the stairs of her house overlooking the sea. Each day she looked for her husband's ship. Nothing appeared.*

"Still, Emily Coffin kept her watch. On the sixth of November 1869, a great gale roared in from the northeast. It pushed a ship straight to-

14

ward the safety of Ragged Cove.

"*Emily Coffin was the first to spot the* Flying Cloud *on the horizon. She and the other towns-people ran out to the beach. Everyone watched nervously. Then, right before their eyes, the horror began. A huge gust of wind broke the mast like a matchstick. In a few seconds, it toppled into the open sea.*"

Jessie paused in her reading to look around the sitting room. Even the grown-ups sat on the edge of their seats. Violet and Benny sat up in their sleeping bags. They hugged their knees to their chests as tightly as they could.

"My goodness, girl!" a guest cried out from a corner of the sitting room. "Get on with the story before we die of suspense."

Jessie went on. "*Everyone on shore watched as the tall mast sank beneath the waves. Only its sail floated across the water like a sheet.*

"*One voice cried above the others: 'To the ship! To the ship! We must row to the ship.'* "

Jessie stopped to catch her breath as if she were one of the very people in the story.

"Keep reading, Jessie," Benny begged. "What happened next?"

"*The* Flying Cloud *tilted sideways. Each gust of wind blew it toward the deadly rocks nearby. Someone on board sent flares into the air, but the blinding rain blew them out.*

"*Eight of the strongest rowers in Ragged Cove jumped into a rowboat. With Emily Coffin shouting from shore, 'Hurry! Hurry!' the rowers tried to beat back the waves. The rain had stopped, but the wind was still strong. Alas, for every inch they gained, they were blown back onto the shore a few feet.*

"*It was hopeless,*" Jessie read, her voice sad. "*And nearly deadly. For one huge wave swamped the bobbing rowboat. All the men went overboard, and the rowboat sank.*"

"Oh, no!" several listeners cried when Jessie got to this part.

"*The men, strong swimmers all, made it back to shore. But there was no cheering. Everyone could see that the* Flying Cloud *was now in great danger. A minute later, a glow came from the broken ship as it drifted ever nearer to the deadly rocks.*

" '*Look, they're trying to signal us!*' *someone onshore screamed.* '*But what can we do while these winds blow against us?*'

"What could they do? The Flying Cloud *was out of reach and listing badly. People talked about the danger of using fire with so much whale oil on board.*

"Another roar went up in the crowd as a huge bonfire appeared over the water. The Flying Cloud *was in flames!*

"Someone cried: 'It's going down! It's sinking!'

" 'Are they lowering the lifeboats?' someone else asked.

" 'It's impossible to see with all the smoke,' another voice answered. 'Let us hope and pray.'

"But their hopes and prayers did not help. The Flying Cloud *disappeared beneath the waves. The horizon was empty again.*

"The townspeople returned to their homes in grief. Only a few people were still at the beach when a young cabin boy named Caleb Plummer made it to shore hours later. He was in shock. He mumbled about the ship being taken over by a sailor named Eli Hull. He died without finishing his story. No one knew what had happened to Captain Coffin or if there had been a mutiny."

Benny tapped Jessie's arm. "Jessie, what's a mutiny?"

"That's when the crew fights against the captain to take over the ship."

"Oh, okay," Benny whispered. "Now you can keep reading."

So Jessie did.

"On stormy days and nights, some people claim to see lights flickering, out where the Flying Cloud *went to its watery grave. Some even say they see a rower on the waves who never reaches the shore. Others hear voices crying along the rocky coast, now called Howling Cliffs. But others say there are no lights, no rowers, no voices, only the sound of the dangerous sea."*

Jessie closed the book.

"Wasn't anyone else found besides the young sailor?" Violet asked.

"No one," answered Mr. Pease, who had just come in. "The ship burned too quickly."

"Did wreckage turn up?" Henry asked.

Mr. Pease shook his head. "A few months after the shipwreck a sealed bottle washed up on the beach. Inside were some pages from Captain Coffin's diary recording all but his last few days. It's a mystery that no one has ever figured out. There are stories about the captain forcing the ship to stay out at sea when it should have returned. And, of course, the sailor's words about a mutiny. But no one really knows what happened."

"What was in those diary pages?" Jessie asked.

Mr. Pease pushed back his own captain's hat and shook his head. "No one knows for sure. You see, out of respect for the captain's widow, Emily Coffin, the pages were turned over to her. She burned them before anyone got to read them. The rest of the diary was never found."

Mrs. Pease, who had been listening from the doorway, spoke to everyone in a soft voice. "Perhaps. Emily Coffin told her children her husband died a hero at sea."

Jessie shivered when a blast of wind hit the Black Dog Inn. "It must have been so dangerous to be at sea if it was anything like tonight. How terrible that so little was saved from the ship."

"Well," Mr. Pease began, "there were a few things besides those pages that washed up — some carvings on whalebone or whale ivory called scrimshaw."

Violet's face brightened. "Oh, yes, we've seen them in museums. Sailors used to carve them with pretty pictures during their long trips away."

Mrs. Pease smiled. "You'll see no prettier scrimshaw than the collection right here in Ragged Cove at the Sailors' Museum. Perhaps you — "

Before Mrs. Pease could finish, Mr. Pease said to his wife, "Now, now. You know how Prudence is." Turning to the children he explained, "She's the curator of the museum. Lately she only allows organized school groups to visit. She wouldn't even let our own grandchildren stop in the last time they came to Ragged Cove."

One of the guests nodded. "That woman doesn't even want adult tourists. Thinks she owns the place, she does!" the woman complained. "Why I have a mind to complain to the town Visitors' Bureau."

Mr. Pease threw up his hands. "I know. I've tried to reason with Prudence. Told her more than once she's going to lose funding for the museum one of these days if she keeps being so stingy with her hours."

Violet looked disappointed. "Oh, dear. I had hoped to see some of those carvings."

"Same here," Henry agreed. "I like to carve things myself and thought I could learn a thing or two. I heard it's the best sailing museum around. We Aldens like anything to do with boats."

"Houseboats, rowboats, sailboats, all boats!" Benny added.

Mr. Pease gave Benny a friendly cuff on the shoulder. "When this mean storm gets tired out, I know Bob Hull will give you a ride on his whale watch boat. That's something you won't forget in a hurry. It may be a few days, though. There'll be major cleaning up to do after this storm — no doubt about that."

"Maybe a treasure from the *Flying Cloud* will wash up onshore, and we'll find it!" Benny declared.

"We know you will!" one guest said with a laugh.

Mr. Pease turned to Benny. "You'll find a

thing or two for sure, my boy. Maybe not from the *Flying Cloud*, of course. But every storm sends in some surprise."

Unlike Benny, Jessie wasn't thinking about surprises. She just couldn't get the *Flying Cloud* out of her mind. "I do wish we knew what was written on those pages that Emily Coffin burned."

Mrs. Pease went over to the bookcase next to the fireplace. She pulled down an old gray book and handed it to Jessie. "Maybe you'll get an idea from this."

"What is it?" Jessie asked.

"A much longer book about the *Flying Cloud*."

Jessie opened to the title page. In beautiful old-fashioned letters it said: *The True Story of the Flying Cloud by Prudence Coffin*. "The museum curator wrote this?" Jessie asked.

"Yes. Prudence Coffin is the great-granddaughter of Captain Jeremiah Coffin and Emily Coffin," Mrs. Pease explained. "She wrote this account of the *Flying Cloud*, based on her great-grandmother's family stories, which were passed down."

"Humph!" one of the guests said. "And my father is King Neptune!"

Benny's eyes were like big blue saucers. "He is? Really?"

Even Violet laughed at this. "Not really, Benny. She's exaggerating."

"Not half as much as that Miss Coffin," the woman went on. "She thinks the Coffins are the only family worth anything in these parts. She claims my ancestor, Eli Hull, led a mutiny against Captain Coffin! And now she's going around saying that my great-nephew, Bob Hull, is no better than a pirate! She's trying to ruin his whale watch business with her stories."

"There, there, Miss Blue," Mrs. Pease said to calm down the woman before she spoiled the evening. "Here, have another johnnycake and cup of tea."

Mrs. Pease's delicious "Bennycakes" worked their magic and quieted the woman. The Aldens, though, were more curious than ever. What was the *real* story of the *Flying Cloud*?

CHAPTER 3

Windows Rattle

By six o'clock in the morning, rays of sunlight squeezed through the shutters. It was warm in the sitting room. The heat was on again. Henry was sound asleep right next to the Peases' dog, Blackie.

"Shh, Benny," Mrs. Pease said when she came in to check on her sleeping guests. "The electricity and heat came back on at four. We told Henry to leave the fire and get some sleep in his own bed upstairs. But he wouldn't leave you children. He's been sleeping on the floor for two hours."

25

"Well he won't be sleeping much longer. Look!" Benny cried.

Blackie was licking Henry's face and making the same kind of whining noises Watch always made to get the Aldens up.

"It's too early, Watch," Henry mumbled when he felt the dog's wet nose on his face. "Go back to sleep."

The Aldens and the other guests couldn't help laughing.

"Here, boy, here," Jessie called to Blackie.

The dog trotted over to Jessie and looked up at her. She patted his smooth, black forehead. "I'll take you outside."

The word "outside" was magic. Just like Watch, Blackie raced around in circles while Jessie got his leash.

"I guess all dogs are the same," Benny laughed.

"And I guess two hours is all the sleep I'm going to get," Henry said, yawning.

The Peases urged their guests to go back to their rooms for real sleep. It was no use. Everyone wanted to see what damage the storm had done.

"Let's get dressed," Benny said. "I want to see the ocean!"

"Wouldn't you like some breakfast first?" Mrs. Pease asked.

"Wow! I almost forgot!" Benny answered.

The Aldens sat down to breakfast when Jessie came back with Blackie. "The town needs volunteers to help with the clean-up," she told everyone. "There are branches and papers and things blown all over. Anyone who wants to help should meet down at the beach in half an hour."

"I'd better have some seconds on those Bennycakes," Benny said. "Cleaning up a whole town is going to make me hungry!"

The minute they had finished, the Aldens said good-bye to their grandfather and raced through the old, narrow streets.

"Everything is blown all over the place," Violet said when she looked around.

Ragged Cove did look a bit topsy-turvy. Store signs were hanging crookedly from buildings. Window boxes had smashed onto the streets.

"Looks like the whole town is here," Jessie

said when the children reached the crowded beach and docks.

Owners were busy putting their boats back into the water. Mr. Pease was holding a clipboard. A younger man in a blue sailor cap handed out big black trash bags and work gloves to the volunteers.

Mr. Pease waved to the Aldens. "Come over here and meet Captain Bob. He's organizing the litter crew. Captain Bob, meet the Aldens — Henry, Jessie, Violet, and Benny. Best crew you could ever have."

"Welcome aboard," the young man said.

Mr. Pease teased Captain Bob. "Now don't talk boat-talk today, Bob. Not unless you want to upset this crew. They were counting on a whale watch ride on the *Jonah* during their visit."

The young man's smile suddenly disappeared. "No boat rides anytime soon," he told the children.

This didn't stop Benny Alden. "You don't know how fast we work. We can get everything shipshape today. Then maybe could we go for a boat ride?"

Captain Bob shook his head. "Sorry, I have to drive up the coast with my truck tomorrow, once we get Ragged Cove in shape. I can't see my way clear for awhile."

Benny was about to speak until he saw Henry give him a look. He knew what that look meant: Button up, Benny!

With some of the other volunteers, the Aldens set off through Ragged Cove with a street map, trash bags, some work gloves, and brooms.

"I never cleaned a town before," Benny said, sounding as if he were on a treasure hunt instead of a clean-up. "Maybe we'll find something."

The Aldens found lots of things. Wet newspapers, boxes, bottles, even a sandy old sneaker went into a garbage bag. Then the children fanned out through the town to gather up the broken branches that were lying everywhere.

By afternoon, their group was finished with their work. They reported back to the beach where Captain Bob was directing a group of teenagers raking the sand.

"What else can we do?" Henry asked the captain.

Captain Bob pushed back his cap. "Unless you can drive a pick-up truck, not much else. We're shipshape here."

Benny tugged on the captain's sleeve. "You think you'll take your whale watching boat out tomorrow?"

Jessie tried to shush Benny, but she was too late.

Again, the man looked upset when Benny mentioned the boat. "I told you, I have work up the coast to do. I won't be going out on my boat for awhile."

Benny pulled down his sailor cap and tried not to get upset. "Sorry," he apologized.

Captain Bob turned away from the children. He didn't seem to want the Aldens bothering him.

Henry handed over the work gloves, brooms, and extra bags without saying anything to Captain Bob. He turned to his brother: "Come on, Benny. Violet had a good idea in the middle of the night. Let's see if we can find the grave of the lost sailor from the *Flying Cloud*. Wouldn't that be interesting?"

Captain Bob spun around and faced the children again. "Why don't you kids get going — I've got work to do."

Henry's eyebrows went up.

"All right, Captain Bob," Jessie said softly.

The Aldens slowly walked toward the town. They didn't say anything right away. All of them were puzzled.

Benny kicked sand every few steps. "Why did Captain Bob get angry after we did a good job?"

Jessie shook her head. "I don't know, Benny. Maybe he was up working all night and got in a bad mood."

Henry put his arm around his younger brother. "Maybe he's upset about losing business because of the storm. Mr. Pease seems to like him, so let's not say anything. Jessie might be right that he's just in a bad mood from working too hard."

"What about what that guest said about Captain Bob last night?" Violet asked.

Henry walked along. "You mean that the

museum curator says Captain Bob is no better than a pirate? That's probably just a lot of talk."

Violet turned around to take another look at Captain Bob. He was off in the distance putting up benches that had blown over. "I think it's a lot of talk, too. Maybe somebody he loves is buried in the cemetery and thinking of them upset him."

Henry smiled at his sister. "Maybe you're right. We'll be careful and respectful while we're there."

The children strolled toward a bluff that overlooked the town and the beach. Beach plum bushes lined the small road that led up to the cemetery.

The Aldens were quiet in this special spot. The cemetery looked very old. Many of the words on the gravestones were worn away by time and weather.

"It's pretty here," Violet said quietly. "You can see the town and the ocean in every direction."

The children walked to the very top of the bluff. The oldest stones were there. They stopped in front of a section marked off by a rusting fence. A sign on it said: COFFIN FAMILY PLOT.

Jessie read some of the granite markers. "Oh look! There's Emily Coffin's gravestone — 1844–1879. She only lived ten years after her husband drowned."

"It's so sad that he drowned at sea. They couldn't be buried next to each other," Violet said softly. "There's an empty space between her grave and their children's graves."

The Aldens were silent for a few minutes. The wind had died down. They listened to the faint breeze blowing through the beach grass that surrounded the gravestones.

Jessie walked away first. In a minute she found what she was looking for. She waved her brothers and sister over.

"Here it is." She pointed to a small, half buried gravestone. "Caleb Plummer. 1855–1869. A brave young sailor, too late to save his ship."

"Isn't that the name in the book you read last night?" Henry asked.

Jessie nodded sadly. "Yes. He was fourteen, just like you, Henry. Everyone thought he rowed to shore to get help for the *Flying Cloud*. But he was too late."

The children took one another's hands. The sun was going down. Out in the cove they could see the boaters returning to the docks. A little farther out, they saw a dark figure rowing to shore.

"It's time to leave," Henry said quietly.

The children turned away from the graves of Caleb Plummer and Emily Coffin. They made their way back to town without a word and without seeing that the little rowboat had disappeared.

CHAPTER 4

Go Away!

Golden sunlight poured into the Crow's Nest as the Aldens awakened.

Jessie tiptoed to the big windows to feel the sun. She opened the doors that led to the widow's walk. "Mmm, fresh sea air."

"Do you see any land yet?" Henry joked. "I dreamed we were on a long sea voyage."

Jessie focused the telescope the Peases left by the window. "I see lots of land with lots of people," she answered, laughing. Then she stopped. "Hey, come here, Henry. Isn't that Captain Bob out on the *Jonah?*"

Henry jumped out of bed to take a look. "It sure is. I thought he said he was driving up the coast today. Do you suppose he's running his whale watch trips after all?"

"If he is, let's get down to the dock," Jessie said. "A sign said the trips leave at eight. We've only got half an hour."

Henry and Jessie tickled Benny and Violet to get them out of bed.

"Why are we rushing?" Violet said, rubbing her eyes.

"Captain Bob is out on his boat," Henry told his sister. "We want to see if he's going out to watch whales today."

"Whales! Did somebody say 'whales'?" Benny cried.

The children left a note under the door of their grandfather's room and went downstairs to tell Mrs. Pease their plans.

She shook her head. "I'll pack a few muffins for the trip. But I don't think the *Jonah* is scheduled for any whale watches today. Mr. Pease said Captain Bob had other plans for the next few days. We've never figured out where he disappears to after every big storm."

"Well, we're going to try, just in case," Benny said hopefully.

Mrs. Pease handed Benny a cloth napkin filled with warm muffins for the trip.

The children ran through the sleepy streets of Ragged Cove and down to the town dock. Sure enough, the Aldens could hear the *Jonah*'s motor warming up. They raced down the dock to the bright blue boat.

"Captain Bob! Captain Bob!" Henry yelled, nearly out of breath.

Jessie whispered to Henry. "Do you think one of us should go on board and see if he's down below? Maybe he didn't hear us."

Jessie didn't wait for Henry's answer. She walked cautiously up the gangplank then walked on deck. Before she got very far, a voice boomed out.

"What are you doing on this boat?" Captain Bob yelled when he came up from the engine room.

Jessie jumped back and caught herself on the railing. "We came to see if you were taking people out whale watching after all."

Captain Bob's face grew red. He seemed

about to shout until he saw that he was scaring the children. He looked down at his boots and shook his head. "I'm not going out today. Told you kids that. Now off you go."

Jessie didn't argue. She walked down the gangplank and away from the *Jonah* with her brothers and sister.

"Maybe another day," Captain Bob called out. "Just not today."

"Let's go sit up on a bench and have breakfast," Henry suggested. "We'll try to come up with some better plans."

But coming up with better plans wasn't easy. It was such a sunny, warm day. Nothing seemed nearly as much fun as whale watching. Jessie unwrapped the napkin full of muffins. The children each took one but only nibbled at the edges. They watched Captain Bob untie the *Jonah* then slowly steer it out of the protected cove.

"Look, he's heading north, up the coast," Henry pointed out. "Not straight out to sea. Maybe he decided to take the boat up the coast instead of taking his truck like he told us yesterday."

"He'd better be careful," Violet said. "Howling Cliffs is in that direction. Mr. Pease said there are lots of boat wrecks up that way."

Benny tossed crumbs of muffins to the seagulls that had discovered the Aldens. "What are we going to do today, Henry?" he asked his older brother.

"Maybe we can visit the Sailors' Museum," Henry said. "Even if we can't go on a whale watching boat, we can go look at pictures and souvenirs of boats at the museum."

Violet was worried. "What if that woman, Miss Coffin, won't let us in? Mr. Pease said she doesn't even like grown-ups visiting."

"We'll try, just in case," Jessie said. "I'd like to see some scrimshaw and sea paintings."

"If I can't be on the sea, at least I'll get to look at a painting of it," Benny said.

The other children laughed, but they agreed with Benny.

CHAPTER 5

A Parrot with a Secret

The Aldens made their way slowly past the quaint shops that lined the cobblestone streets of Ragged Cove. They headed to a big white captain's house with a huge black ship's anchor planted in front.

"Looks like this is it," Henry said when he saw the sign for the Sailors' Museum. "Not exactly busy."

"Not exactly open, either," Jessie said.

She stepped up to the door and rapped on the brass door knocker. While the children waited for someone to open up, Benny peeked in the window by the door.

"There's somebody inside. A lady with gray hair, I think. She's just standing there," Benny told Jessie. "Knock again."

Jessie did. She rapped nearly a dozen times before the door opened just a crack.

"No children allowed without an adult," an old voice said from the inside.

This didn't stop Jessie Alden. "But . . . the sign here says the adult can be fourteen or over. Our brother Henry is fourteen."

Benny scooted by Jessie and looked up at the woman. "We know about your great-grandfather and his boat, the *Flying Cloud*. And we saw your great-grandmother's gravestone. And Jessie read us a story about your family."

A tiny smile passed over the woman's face.

Benny took a deep breath. "We like whales and boats, and Violet knows how to paint pictures of the ocean. And Henry can carve anything, even a whale tooth. If we ever find one."

The door opened a few more inches. "Well, I don't know. Most children come in here and go out disappointed. I have nothing here but old things, not even a gift shop."

"We make our own gifts," Violet said proudly. "But maybe we can get some ideas from your museum."

The woman liked Violet's idea very much. She waved the children inside.

Henry spoke first. "We're the Aldens, Miss Coffin. We're staying at the Black Dog Inn with our grandfather. The Peases told us about you. This is Jessie and Violet and Benny, and I'm Henry."

The woman seemed curious and turned to Jessie. "I see. Tell me how you happened to be reading my book, young lady."

"Well, first I read a story called 'Watery Grave: The Wreck of the *Flying Cloud*.' "

The woman stiffened and looked angry. "That! I thought you meant the true history I wrote. That other story is just a lot of lies and gossip!"

Jessie wasn't quite sure what to say next. She didn't want to upset Miss Coffin. "Oh, but then Mrs. Pease gave me your book, and I read some of it last night. It's so sad."

Miss Coffin got a faraway look. "Yes, it is a sad story. So many died, so close to home. But there's something worse than that."

"What could be worse?" Violet asked.

"Humph," the woman began. "What's worse is what caused the tragedy of the *Flying Cloud*. There was an attempted . . . well, never mind."

"Mutiny?" Benny asked, proud to show off his new word.

"Yes, but it was just that crazy Eli Hull," Miss Coffin said. "Why, my great-grandfather was one of the most beloved sea captains in these parts. He treated his crew like his own family. Anybody who knows anything knows that! His crew would never have turned against him."

"Of course not," Violet said softly. She was reading the sign on a glass cabinet filled with carvings. "Anybody can see that Captain Coffin's crew loved him. Look at all this scrimshaw his sailors carved for him. Were all these pieces in your family, Miss Coffin?"

Violet's question perked up Miss Coffin right away. "Why yes — yes, they were. You see the crew made these carvings for my great-grandfather to give to his wife and children. Aren't they the prettiest things? Here, let me unlock the cabinet so you can see how clever these carvings really are."

Miss Coffin fished into her pocket and pulled out the key to the cabinet. "Which piece would you like to look at first?" she asked Violet.

Violet pointed to a whale tooth about six inches tall. On it was a parrot carving that was colored in with blue ink. "That one."

"That's my favorite, too," Miss Coffin said. "It's a picture of Gabby, the pet parrot my great-grandfather rescued on a voyage to South America. Its wing was broken, and he nursed the bird back to health. Gabby traveled on many of my great-grandfather's voyages."

Violet and Benny looked upset, remembering what had happened to his last voyage.

"There, there," Miss Coffin said, "believe it or not, we think somebody freed Gabby

from his cage right before the *Flying Cloud* went up in flames. Gabby flew right back to my great-grandparents' house. And, believe it or not, I remember Gabby myself. He lived a long, long time after my great-grandparents died. We think Gabby was nearly sixty years old when he died of old age."

Benny was amazed. "Sixty! That's almost as old as our grandfather."

"Did Gabby talk?" Jessie asked.

"Did he *talk*? Why he never stopped talking!" Miss Coffin answered proudly. "He said: 'Cap Coff, Cap Coff' over and over every day until he died. He meant Captain Coffin, of course, my great-grandfather. Anyway, one of my great-grandfather's crew carved this piece of scrimshaw in happier days, when the *Flying Cloud* was the most successful whaling ship in these parts."

"Did the parrot know how to say anything else?" Benny asked. He was still amazed that parrots lived such a long time.

" 'Hardtack, hardtack' was something else he was always shrieking. Do you children know what hardtack is?"

Jessie smiled. "I do. It's dried, hard-baked bread that sailors took on long voyages. Dried bread kept better and didn't get full of mold."

"Good for you, young lady," Miss Coffin said. "The crew would put pieces of hardtack in soup or tea. Gabby just loved hardtack."

Benny said, "I bet Bennycakes are better. That's what Miss Pease calls johnnycakes, because I eat so many!"

This seemed to please Miss Coffin very much. "Those are my favorites, too."

The children walked around the small museum and admired the ships' models, paintings, and the many gadgets from whaling ships. They stopped before a display case of old photographs.

Miss Coffin pointed to a picture of a little girl standing with some older people. Off to the side was a cage with a parrot.

"That's me with my grandparents," Miss Coffin said. "And there's Gabby himself. You know, I do have something you children would like."

Miss Coffin went to a bookcase. She pulled

out a children's book called *Gabby, the Parrot Who Couldn't Stop Talking*.

"Benny, Violet, take this as a present. It's out of print now. We used to sell it in the museum," Miss Coffin said. "I wrote it many years ago when children wanted to know about the great days of the *Flying Cloud*."

Benny and Violet looked through the little book. They stopped at a page near the end that listed all the words Gabby knew how to say. "What did 'capsick, capsick' mean?"

Miss Coffin shook her head. "My family never figured that one out. Drove us crazy with that word. My great-grandfather was never sick a day in his life, certainly not seasick."

"I hope I'm like Captain Coffin," Benny said, "and that I don't get seasick when we go out whale watching."

Miss Coffin's blue eyes darkened. "Whale watching? When are you going to do that?"

Benny didn't like the way Miss Coffin was looking at him now. Something about whale watching seemed to upset the old woman.

"We . . . we don't know," Jessie said before

Benny said anything else. "We're hoping Captain Bob will take us out on the *Jonah* in the next few days. We are interested in whales and how they live and how to save them."

"Humph," Miss Coffin said. "Well, you don't need to go on that man's boat to find out about whales. Everything you could ever want to know about them is in this library." She stopped. "And it's a much safer way to learn than getting on a boat with that . . . that careless captain. Captain indeed!"

"But we want to see whales swimming," Benny said before he could catch himself, "not just read about them."

Miss Coffin stood up and walked to the front door. "Then I can't be of any further help to you. Now I'll have to ask you to leave. I've a busload of tourists — *adults* — coming this afternoon, and I need to get the museum ready. I think I'll need that book back, Miss. It turns out I don't have enough copies after all."

Violet handed back the little book about Gabby. "Here. I guess we'll go now," she said to Miss Coffin. "Thank you very much for the tour. Can we come back again to look at the whale books you mentioned?"

Miss Coffin wouldn't look at Violet or the other Aldens. "I'll be too busy. There are several tours I have to organize this week. I can't say for sure what the museum hours will be for the next few days."

With that, Miss Coffin led the children to the front door and let them out.

"Do you think Miss Coffin is worried that whale watching trips harm the whales?" Jessie asked Henry. "She got so upset when we said we wanted to go on one of Captain Bob's trips."

Henry was just as puzzled as the other children. "The boat rides don't get close enough to disturb the whales."

Benny was the most upset of all. "Is . . . is the *Jonah* safe, Henry?" he asked.

"I'm sure it is," Henry said. "Mr. Pease told Grandfather that Captain Bob was in the Coast Guard and knows everything there is to know about boats. And whales, too. Miss Coffin just doesn't like Captain Bob because he's related to Eli Hull."

CHAPTER 6

A Mysterious Box

The Aldens spent the next morning at the beach. Benny hunted on his hands and knees for sharks' teeth. Violet searched for pretty beach glass and unbroken shells, while Jessie and Henry scouted for driftwood. The whole time the Aldens were on the beach, they kept an eye on the *Jonah*.

"It looks like Captain Bob is going out on his boat again," Jessie sighed. "I wonder why he isn't taking anyone with him. It's another perfect day."

"It sure is," Henry agreed. "At breakfast

Grandfather and Mr. Pease said maybe we could go for a boat ride on the *Sea Dog* when they're not so busy. But it's not the same as a whale boat."

Benny walked up to Henry empty-handed. "I didn't find one single shark tooth. Just some broken shells and this skinny old gull feather."

Henry took the feather and stuck it on Benny's sailor cap. "We'll call you Macaroni!" Henry joked.

Benny smiled and went over to a bench to watch the boats. Soon the other children joined him. They spread out their handful of sand dollars, shells, and driftwood.

"Maybe this afternoon, we can get some glue and make some pretty things out of what we collected," Violet suggested.

Henry looked out at the *Jonah*. "I wish we could convince Captain Bob to take us out on a whale watch."

"What if I went and asked him about a ride?" Benny asked. "Maybe he's in a good mood today. I'll offer him one of Mrs. Pease's muffins."

The three older children looked at each other.

"All right, go ahead," Jessie said with a smile. "But if he gets angry, come right back."

"I will!" Benny cried before he raced off.

Down at the dock, Captain Bob was untying ropes. The motor of the *Jonah* was already humming. The captain was so busy, he didn't see Benny right away.

As soon as the captain looked up, Benny was ready. "I brought you some muffins. You might get hungry wherever you're going. Here." Benny held out the napkin-wrapped muffins.

"No, thanks. I've eaten," Captain Bob mumbled.

"You can save them for lunch," Benny suggested.

The captain shook his head. "No, thanks. I brought my lunch."

"Where're you going?" Benny asked. "Whale watching?"

Captain Bob shook his head. "I told you, son, no whale watching for a few days. I've got other things to do first.''

Benny finally gave up and turned around. He walked down the dock slowly, one small step after another.

"Hey, Benny," the captain called out. "Come back!"

Benny whirled around and skipped back to the boat. "What?"

"Listen," the captain said. "Give me a couple days, then I promise I'll take you out to see some whales. How's that?"

Benny wanted to smile, but there was nothing to smile about. "I don't think we'll be here. My grandfather is almost finished with his business at the fish-packing plant. Then we're driving home."

The captain stared over Benny's head at the other Aldens. "What are your brother and sisters doing right now?"

"Sorting out stuff we found on the beach," Benny answered. "I was looking for sharks' teeth, but I didn't find any."

The captain thought for a minute. "Look, run over and get your brother and sisters. I'll take you out for a quick ride now. Can't get in much whale watching, but maybe we can go out looking for wreckage."

Benny's big blue eyes got even bigger. "Is that the same as treasures?"

"Kind of," Captain Bob answered. "I'm headed out to Howling Cliffs. Lots of things wash up there after big storms."

Benny's eyes widened when he heard this. "Howling Cliffs? Goody!" He raced off to tell everyone about Captain Bob's offer.

The Aldens were ready to board the *Jonah* in no time.

"Climb aboard then," the captain told the children. "I guess I could use some extra hands where I'm going."

A few tourists were on the shore, so the Aldens waved to them as if they were going on a long sea voyage.

Ragged Cove grew smaller and smaller in the distance. Overhead, seagulls followed the little blue boat. Benny threw out pieces of muffin for the hungry birds but saved a few pieces for himself.

"Sea air sure makes birds hungry," he said with a laugh.

"And any kind of air makes *you* hungry!" Henry joked.

This was the first time the children heard Captain Bob laugh. Now he seemed glad to have the Aldens aboard.

When the muffins were gone, Benny walked to the front of the *Jonah* to see where they were headed. "Hey, what are all those big gray rubber things up ahead?"

"Whale off! Whale off!" Captain Bob yelled. "Here, take a look through these binoculars, Benny."

"Wow!" Benny cried. "It's a bunch of whales!"

The captain laughed. "Not a bunch, Benny, a pod. A bunch of whales is called a pod. And when we see them, we yell 'Whale off!' just like in the old whaling days."

"Whale off! Whale off!" Benny yelled. "Look, some of them are looking above the water."

Indeed, three or four shiny gray whales seemed to be peeking above the waterline as they swam in their pod.

"Now they're spyhopping," Captain Bob

told Benny. "That means they're staying just above the water to keep an eye on us. They don't want us to get too close. I'm going to steer away so we don't frighten them."

The children couldn't take their eyes off the beautiful creatures, especially Violet. "They're so graceful for such big animals. I wish it weren't so splashy, or I'd take out my sketchbook."

The whale pod swam farther out to sea. Captain Bob piloted the *Jonah* up the coastline toward some tall gray cliffs. There the wind blew hard against the children's faces. There were no whales and no other boats to be seen. When Captain Bob slowed down and steered into the wind, the children heard a strange sound.

"Is that crying?" Violet asked.

The children listened and looked up at Captain Bob. His sky blue eyes looked straight ahead as he carefully guided the *Jonah* through the jagged rocks. The sound grew louder.

"This is Howling Cliffs," Captain Bob said without once taking his eyes off the dangerous rocks. "The wind always makes funny sounds near these rocks."

In a whispery voice, Violet spoke up. "Jessie read us a story about that sound. Some people say that's the sound of the sailors' voices calling for help when the *Flying Cloud* went down."

"Yes, some say that," Captain Bob answered as he piloted the boat to a small, protected beach.

"This looks like a secret beach. I bet nobody has cleaned it up yet," Violet said in an excited voice, once they were ashore. "Bring the fishing bags from the boat, Jessie. There are lots of shells and driftwood to collect."

"Even a horseshoe crab shell!" Benny cried when he spotted one. "Now I have one treasure already. Do you think we'll find some more, Captain Bob?"

"I hope so," the captain said. "I like to see what washes up after a storm. I couldn't get in here yesterday because I missed low tide. I hope nothing valuable was washed away."

"Me, too," Benny said. "I'm going to climb

those rocks. Maybe that's where pirates hid their treasures."

"Go ahead, Benny," Captain Bob said. "I'll be up on some of the higher ledges. See you in a while."

"I think Captain Bob is just shy, that's all," Violet said after the captain left.

Henry agreed. "And he's a very careful pilot. Did you see the way he steered the *Jonah* right around those sharp rocks? I wonder why Miss Coffin thought he wasn't a safe sailor."

"Can I climb these rocks, Jessie?" Benny asked. "There may be some treasures up there."

"Go ahead, Benny," Jessie said.

Benny climbed up the rocks to a wide ledge. "I like it up here," he yelled down. "I can see all over."

Benny explored the ledge. Overhead a sea bird was screaming. Benny soon figured out why. "Hey, there's a bunch of nests hidden in these big holes in the rocks. They're like little caves."

"Well, come down soon, so the mother

bird doesn't get upset," Violet told Benny.

"Okay, okay, I'm coming," Benny said. "I just want to get this piece of wood that's sticking out from some rocks."

Benny reached into a hole in the rocks to grab a thick wedge of wood. "Ugh, ugh," he said, pulling hard. "This old piece of wood is stuck."

By this time Captain Bob was standing right above Benny on another ledge. "What've you got there, Benny?"

"A stuck piece of wood," Benny said, all red in the face and out of breath. "I want to see what it is. Maybe somebody poked it in here on purpose."

Captain Bob lowered himself down to Benny's ledge. "Okay, Benny, you pull that side, and I'll jiggle this."

Benny and the captain jiggled the wood back and forth. Finally some dirt and rocks came loose along with a big wooden box.

"It's a box!" Benny said in amazement.

"Congratulations, Benny!" Captain Bob said. "You've got good eyes. This box was so well hidden in the rocks, I probably passed it a dozen times without noticing it. Let's get it down to the beach."

"What's that?" Henry asked when Benny and Captain Bob put the box down on the sand.

"It's an old postbox," Captain Bob told the children. "Back in whaling times sailors used to leave mail for each other in boxes they put up around the coastline. Sometimes they sent letters or small scrimshaw carvings for other sailors to send on to their families. A box like this is very rare."

"What about gold coins?" Benny asked.

The captain pried open the box lid with a knife.

Benny's face fell. "Just some old stuff," he said when he saw the blackened spoons and forks and lots of yellowed bone carvings scattered in the box. There was also a small, rusty piece of pipe that was sealed off at both ends.

Violet picked up one of the many carved objects. "Oooh," she said. "These are scrimshaw clothespins. The sailors used to carve them from whalebone for their wives. I read

that on one of the displays at the Sailors' Museum."

"Clothespins? Aw shucks," Benny said.

Captain Bob couldn't help smiling. "I guess old clothespins don't seem too exciting, but I'm sure these have some value."

"What about that rusty iron pipe?" Henry asked.

The captain picked up the length of iron. "It's the end of an old cannon barrel. Sometimes sailors used to put documents inside for protection, then close them up."

"Can I see?" Benny asked.

The captain didn't answer right away. "Yes, uh, sure. But first I have to oil and sand it off on the boat to see if I get it open. Wait here."

"May I watch?" Benny asked. "Maybe there are pirate coins in there."

The captain didn't answer. He headed back to the boat. He didn't seem to want anyone to come along.

Fifteen minutes went by. Captain Bob still hadn't returned with the cannon barrel.

"It's taking Captain Bob an awfully long

time to get that barrel open," Henry said.

"I know," Jessie agreed. "We should probably head back. I told Mrs. Pease we'd be back by lunchtime. I don't want her to get worried."

Violet carefully wrapped up all the other objects in the box. Henry and Benny carried the box onto the *Jonah.*

"I'll go below deck and tell Captain Bob we should go," Jessie said.

"Captain Bob," Jessie whispered. "Did you get the cannon barrel apart?"

"Hhhh!" Captain Bob said, when Jessie surprised him. "I didn't hear you come down. Uh . . . go back up. I'll be there in a minute." The captain quickly wrapped a rag around the cannon barrel.

Jessie could tell Captain Bob didn't seem to want her around. "I'm sorry. It's just that Mrs. Pease is expecting us back at lunchtime, and we don't want to worry her. The cannon barrel, did you get it open?"

Captain Bob put the barrel behind him. "Why . . . uh — no, I didn't. The damp air well . . . uh . . . it just rusted the whole thing shut. Now go on back up."

"Did he find any coins, Jessie, did he?" Benny asked when Jessie returned.

Captain Bob popped up right behind Jessie. "Sorry, Benny. Nothing to report. The thing is stuck good and tight. I'll bring it home to work on it some more."

"Can I take it to the Sailors' Museum?" Benny asked the captain. "The lady there has lots of things like that."

"No," said the captain, his voice suddenly turning unfriendly. "It needs to be cleaned. I know as much about these things as Miss Coffin anyway."

"Doesn't something like this belong in the Sailors' Museum?" Jessie asked.

Seeing how sad Benny looked, Captain Bob softened. "Well, you were the one who found the box," he said. "So if that's what you want to do, then there's nothing else to say. Take it to Miss Coffin." In a few minutes the captain piloted the *Jonah* through the nearby rocks and out to the open sea. He seemed to want to be alone with his thoughts and the crying sounds of Howling Cliffs.

CHAPTER 7

A Stranger Disappears

It was lunchtime when the *Jonah* docked. But the Aldens forgot all about being hungry. They couldn't wait to show Miss Coffin their discoveries.

"I just know she'll be happy to see us when we show her these things," Violet said. "Not like yesterday."

Henry ran ahead to call Mrs. Pease so they could eat lunch later and go to the museum instead. "She's going to leave some sandwiches for us in the refrigerator," Henry told everyone when he came back from making his phone call. "Now we can go straight to the Sailors' Museum to show Miss Coffin what we found. So let's unload everything."

Captain Bob hadn't said a word to the Aldens the whole ride back to Ragged Cove. Still silent, he packed up the wooden postbox along with the other discoveries into a small cart. As he covered everything to protect it, he finally spoke to the children again. "I have work to do on the *Jonah* this afternoon. I can't come to the museum."

"But you have to!" Benny cried. "You helped us find everything."

"It doesn't matter," the captain said. "Miss Coffin will know what to do with all of it. Mind you, go slowly with the cart over the cobbled streets. The postbox is about ready to come apart. Everything else should be fine. You can bring the cart back later and leave it at the dock. I'll find it okay."

"Are you sure you won't come?" Violet asked. "You're the one who made it possible for us to save these things. Wouldn't you like to see what Miss Coffin says? She'll be so happy."

"Not if she sees me," Captain Bob said in a low voice the children could hardly hear.

The Aldens set out for the museum, pulling the cart slowly down the dock and toward Ragged Cove.

"I can't figure out why Captain Bob won't come with us," Jessie said. "It seems silly to be upset about things that happened so long ago."

"Well, he *is* upset, and so is Miss Coffin," Henry told Jessie. "When I told Mrs. Pease we were going to the Sailors' Museum with Captain Bob, she seemed surprised. She said Miss Coffin has had nothing good to say about the captain since he came back to Ragged Cove after the Coast Guard." Henry pulled the cart around the corner carefully. "Mrs. Pease said there's been a feud between the Coffins and Captain Bob's family, the Hulls, ever since the *Flying Cloud*. I guess that's why he didn't want us to take these things to Miss Coffin."

"How sad," said Violet. "Why can't people get along with each other?"

As the Aldens walked past the shops on

Cod Street, Violet stopped in front of a store called Spooner Cooke's Scrimshaw Shop. "I just wanted to see if there were any scrimshaw clothespins like the ones we found in the postbox," Violet said. "But I don't see any. There are some other pretty things, though, even some carved whalebone toys."

The other children crowded up to the window to take a look. Benny stood on his tiptoes and pressed his forehead against the window. Just as he did, a man with a sharp beaky nose and a bald head rushed out of the shop.

"Get away from there, you kids!" the man yelled. "You're smudging my clean windows."

The children jumped back. Henry took the cloth covering the postbox to clean the window. "Sorry," he apologized. "We were just looking at the nice antiques you have."

The man didn't seem to hear what Henry had just said. Instead, his eyes grew wide when he noticed the postbox in the cart. "Where did you get that?" he asked the Aldens in a loud voice.

"We found it out by Howling Cliffs," Jessie answered. "Captain Bob took us out there to see if any wreckage washed up after the storm. My brother found this hidden in some rocks."

Benny peeked out from behind Jessie. "The box was sticking out from the rocks. All it's got in it are old spoons and clothespins and toys made out of bones."

The man reached down for the box. "Let me look at this."

"Sorry, sir," Henry told the man. "These things belong in a museum. That's where we're going right now. An expert needs to look at everything to see if it's valuable."

This made the man very angry. "I'll have you know, young man, that *I* am an expert. Here's my card."

Henry took a business card from the man. On it was an ink drawing of a magnifying glass. The card said: SPOONER COOKE: SCRIM-SHAW DEALER.

"All the same," Henry said after he'd put the card in his pocket, "we're taking these things to the museum. You can check with Miss Coffin."

"Humph," said the man. "Prudence and I have known each other since we were born. I happen to be on the museum board, as you will soon find out. Now you'd better mind how you carry those things along these streets. Imagine, an antique postbox in the hands of a bunch of kids!"

"A pod of kids," Benny said under his breath as the children walked on.

Henry, Jessie, and Violet couldn't help giggling.

"This time, let's go in the back, to the delivery entrance," Jessie advised when they reached the Sailors' Museum. "Then Miss Coffin will have to open the door right away."

Sure enough, as soon as they knocked on the side door marked "Delivery Entrance," Miss Coffin opened it.

"The museum is closed," she told the children.

"That's okay, Miss Coffin," Jessie said. "We came to give you something special for the museum, not to visit."

With that, Henry pulled off the cloth covering the postbox. "Look what we found at Howling Cliffs."

Miss Coffin gasped. "Why it's a sailors' postbox! I thought we'd found the last one a few years ago." She bent down to take a closer look. "I can't believe it hasn't rotted away."

"That's 'cause it was inside some rocks, nice and dry," Benny said proudly. "The same place where bird mothers make nests so they're safe. It's a good hiding place."

Miss Coffin smiled then looked away from the children. "I'm sorry about yesterday," she said. "It's just that . . . that Bob Hull, well, I wish he had never come back to Ragged Cove. His family did enough to spread lies about my great-grandfather. Then he goes talking to the tourists and . . ."

Jessie spoke gently to the old woman. "Captain Bob doesn't spread lies. Truly, Miss Coffin. He's the one who helped us get this box out in one piece. He even packed it up in this cart so we could bring it to the museum."

"That may well be." Miss Coffin paused.

"Let's take a look at what's here. Come in."

The children carefully took the postbox and its wrapped objects inside. They spread them out on a large desk in Miss Coffin's office.

The old woman put on her glasses and walked back and forth. "My, my," she repeated several times. "This is quite a find, quite a find."

The children could see how pleased she was, even with the old banged-up spoons. She showed the children a display case of old dishes and silverware. "Look," she said, "the spoons have the same design."

"I wish some coins had the same design as the one in here," Benny said when he looked into a display case of old money.

"Tsk, tsk," Miss Coffin said without looking up from what she was doing. "Everything here will be valuable to people who are interested in history. Now, I wonder what's under this cloth."

"Just a section of a rusty cannon barrel," Henry said. "Captain Bob tried to get the top off, but it's stuck."

"Oh my! Part of a cannon barrel!" Miss Coffin said, as excited as if the children had brought her a sea chest filled with gold. "We must get it open in case there are any old papers or logbooks inside."

"Yes, Captain Bob said sailors used the barrels to keep their papers dry," Jessie said. "But I don't know if we'll have any luck with this one. Captain Bob tried to oil it up and even used some of his boat tools. It's rusted shut."

Miss Coffin couldn't resist. She put the cannon barrel on its side and twisted the end. "Why, what do you mean? It comes right off!"

And so it did. In a single twist, the end of the barrel was off, as if someone had barely screwed it on.

"That's strange," Jessie said. "Captain Bob said he'd had no luck with it at all."

Henry scratched his head. "I guess it's the same as when a strong person tries to untwist a lid and then gives up. The next person hardly has to turn it at all."

"I'm not so sure of that," Jessie said. She

was puzzled about the way Miss Coffin had managed to open the barrel on the first try.

"Oh, my!" Miss Coffin cried again. "There *are* a few things in here — an old book and some documents." She pulled them out and began examining them.

Benny never gave up. He shook the barrel to see if anything else was inside. "It's empty," he said, disappointed. "Just those old papers."

Miss Coffin gathered up the old, yellowed papers at one end of the table. "Yes, that's all there was in there, just old papers, nothing you children would be interested in."

Jessie stepped forward. "I would like to see some of them, Miss Coffin. May I?"

Miss Coffin seemed a bit nervous. "Well, yes . . . yes, of course. Perhaps tomorrow after I have a chance to look through them. They're so old, they are extremely delicate."

"We'll be careful," Violet said. "We've found old books and papers before, and nothing bad happened to them."

This didn't convince Miss Coffin. She pushed the papers and books down to the far end of the table, away from the Aldens. "If you want to help, why don't you children make a list of all these other things you found? There are toys, scrimshaw clothespins, even these little whalebone pie cutters here. Now those are very special."

"Oh," Violet said, delighted with the delicate object with the little wheel. "Mrs. McGregor has one to cut pie dough. Only hers is wooden and not as pretty as these."

"Yes, they are pretty," said Miss Coffin. "The sailors carved many useful items for their families at home — all kinds of kitchen things, toys for their children. See if any of the pieces you found match what's in those cabinets. Then maybe we can get some idea of who might have carved them. Here's the key to unlock some of the display cases."

Jessie didn't feel right about taking the key. "Don't you want to show us what to do?" she asked Miss Coffin. "Not that we won't be careful. We just want to make sure we take things out properly and know what to look for."

Miss Coffin seemed impatient. "Go. Just

lay the pieces from the cabinet at one end of the table out there and the pieces you found at Howling Cliffs at the other end. Here's a magnifying glass, so you can compare the pieces. Now go!"

The children stood there for a moment without moving. Why was Miss Coffin rushing them?

"Let's go to the main room," Henry said. "We might as well get started."

Henry and Jessie unlocked the first scrimshaw cabinet and carefully took out a tray of carvings. Benny and Violet laid out the pieces they had found on a felt-covered table.

"I guess we should just do what she says," Jessie whispered. "I did want to see what some of those papers were, though. I was hoping there might be some new information about what happened to Captain Coffin and the *Flying Cloud*."

Violet defended the old woman. "Maybe since the papers might have something to do with her great-grandfather, she just wants to look at them by herself first."

The children sat down to work. Violet especially enjoyed handling the delicate little whalebone pictures, tools, and toys. "Look," she cried, holding up a small whalebone picture carved with a parrot. "I bet this is another picture of Gabby. These pieces must be from the *Flying Cloud*!"

Jessie studied the small, flat carving they had found in the postbox. She compared it to the museum's whale tooth carving of the parrot. "The parrot has the same markings. Let's go show this to Miss Coffin."

The Aldens raced into Miss Coffin's office without even bothering to knock. The old woman jumped up when the children burst in all excited.

"We found a picture of Gabby, look!" Violet cried. "See they're the same."

If the children were expecting Miss Coffin to be thrilled, they were disappointed. Miss Coffin didn't seem at all curious about the carvings. She hardly seemed to realize the Aldens had all crowded into her office.

"Yes, I see," she said. She barely looked at what Violet was showing her.

Jessie stared at Miss Coffin's desk then

checked under it. "Is something missing here, Miss Coffin?" she asked the old woman. "Wasn't there an old leather book with all these other papers?"

Miss Coffin looked away from the children. After taking a deep breath she finally answered Jessie's question. "This is everything. There wasn't any book, just these letters and such."

"But, but — " Jessie began until Miss Coffin shushed her.

"Now come out to the front room and show me what you children have found," Miss Coffin said, rushing the children from her office.

The Aldens could hardly keep up with the old woman. Jessie turned around to make sure there wasn't a small book somewhere in all the papers. She didn't see a thing.

Miss Coffin looked over the pieces on the table. The children hoped she would be happy to see how closely the pieces matched. But the old woman barely seemed interested.

"Put everything away now," she told the children.

At that moment, everyone felt a draft of sea air blow through the museum. The door to the delivery area banged.

"Hey, I think you got a delivery, Miss Coffin," Henry said. "I just saw someone in a blue sailor hat go by."

Miss Coffin went to the back office again. The old documents and papers were scattered on the table along with some of the other pieces from the postbox.

"Did the wind blow these things around?" Jessie asked. "Is anything missing?"

Miss Coffin looked terribly upset. "You see, there's too much confusion with everyone here. I simply must ask you to leave so I can organize these things without distraction."

Benny swallowed hard. "We'll be quiet."

"Yes, we will," Jessie said. "We would just like to get a closer look at all the things Benny found, that's all."

"Well, you'll have to come back tomorrow, then," Miss Coffin said. "I don't feel up to the job right now. I need some peace and quiet. Now please go back to the inn."

The Aldens could see Miss Coffin had made up her mind. They were almost sorry they had brought the postbox to her at all. They left without another word.

"All I wanted to do was spread everything out like we always do when we find things," Benny said as they walked down the alley next to the museum. "That's all. Hey, who's that?"

A man in a blue sailor cap stepped from a doorway and ran down the alleyway, ahead of the children.

"He's got a hat just like Captain Bob's," Henry noticed. "But I'm not sure he's that tall. I can't tell."

The Aldens quickly raced to the street. Whoever had been in the alleyway had melted in to the crowd of tourists. Many of them were wearing the same blue sailor hats sold in all the souvenir shops in Ragged Cove.

CHAPTER 8

A Friend Disappears

The next morning, in the dining room, Mrs. Pease bustled around the Aldens' table like a mother hen. "Now today I want you children to eat well and not run off with just a few muffins. Especially you, Benny."

"I won't," said Benny who was on his second helping of scrambled eggs.

"And I can't have my guests just making do with a few sandwiches like yesterday, either," Mrs. Pease told the children. "With all your adventures, you need a proper lunch.

Today it's my special clam chowder with apple pie for dessert."

Mr. Alden put down his coffee cup. "Don't worry, Mrs. Pease. We'll all be here for lunch today, that I promise. My grandchildren are going to show me all the treasures they found and took to the Sailors' Museum. Then we're going to see whether we can go out on Captain Bob's boat."

"Oh, I hope you're not counting on that," Mrs. Pease said. "Captain Bob told Mr. Pease he won't be starting up for awhile. I must say that puzzles me on these fine days. Still, that's always the way with him after a big storm."

"We'll go check anyway, after we visit with Miss Coffin, that is," Mr. Alden said.

Mrs. Pease refilled Mr. Alden's cup with steaming coffee. "I am so glad your grandchildren have made friends with Prudence. And to think they found such treasures! Why it's just the thing Prudence needs. She spends too much time locked up in that museum and worrying about things that happened a long time ago that can't be changed. It's good for her to have some young people around."

Jessie took a sip of her juice and looked up at Mrs. Pease. "I'm not so sure about that, Mrs. Pease. She didn't seem too happy with us yesterday afternoon."

"She practically shooed us out of the museum," Benny said, still hurt about that.

"Museum? Are you talking about the theft at the Sailors' Museum?" a guest at the next table asked, when he heard what the Aldens were talking about. He held up his morning newspaper. A headline in large letters said: SCRIMSHAW THEFT AT SAILORS' MUSEUM.

"May we look at that?" Jessie asked the guest. "We were just at the museum yesterday. We didn't know anything was stolen."

"Happened last night," the guest told Jessie. "Whoever took the carvings knew what was valuable. Two of the oldest, rarest pieces were taken."

The Aldens, with Mrs. Pease looking over their shoulders, read the article.

"Oh, no!" Violet cried. "It says the whale tooth with the parrot carving was taken. Oh, I wonder if the parrot picture we found was taken, too!"

Henry grabbed a piece of toast. "Come on. Let's get over there!"

In no time the children were at the front door of the Sailors' Museum. One of the Ragged Cove police officers was there, knocking on the door and looking in the windows.

"Sorry kids, it's closed," the officer said. "You'll have to come back another time. Early this morning, Miss Coffin reported a robbery, so we're sealing off the scene of the crime. I was just trying to get Miss Coffin to open up, but she doesn't seem to be around."

"She's not?" Henry said. "She told us to come back to help out with some of the old things we found at Howling Cliffs. Did you try the delivery entrance?"

"I did," the officer answered. "She's gone, though her car is here. Did you happen to see anything unusual at the museum yesterday?"

"Everything was fine when we left yesterday afternoon," Henry said.

"Except for the man in the blue sailor hat," Benny broke in. "The one who passed us in the alleyway, right there."

The officer bent down to talk to Benny. "Tell me something. Did you ever see the man before?"

"Maybe we did," Benny said, trying to think. "The hat anyway. See, I have one just like it, only smaller."

"Well, I wish that hat was more of a clue. It seems anybody around here who ever set foot on a boat wears a blue sailor hat like that.

"Maybe later when my partner comes back you can help identify what else might be missing," the police officer said. "Miss Coffin was so upset when she called. She wasn't able to give us much information about what was gone — just said some scrimshaw. We don't really know about anything else. It doesn't help that she isn't here to let us in. We have to get a spare key from the town hall."

While the officer was talking, Benny spotted a familiar face looking down from a building across the street. He waved, but the face disappeared from the window.

"Who's that, Benny?" Jessie asked. She

looked up at the deserted building.

"Captain Bob. At least it looked like Captain Bob," Benny answered. "He was looking at us. If it was him, I mean."

"Bob Hull?" the officer said. "Oh, I don't think so. He's busy getting the *Jonah* ready for a whale watch this afternoon. I ran into him down at the docks. He's got a big tourist group scheduled."

Violet looked a bit upset. "I wonder why he didn't tell the Peases. In fact, he told them he wasn't going out for a few days."

"Well, all I can think is that he's got a busload down from Bassville," the officer said. "Maybe he's only taking groups today."

"But we're a group," Violet said. "We wanted to go out with our grandfather before we leave Ragged Cove in a couple days. Grandfather was looking forward to it."

"There's something else we can do, Violet. Follow me," Jessie said all of a sudden. "See you later, officer."

Jessie pulled away her brothers and sister and began walking toward the street with all the shops.

"Where are we going, Jessie?" Violet wanted to know.

Jessie turned down a narrow cobbled street. "Spooner Cooke's Scrimshaw Shop."

Henry smacked his forehead. "I was thinking that very thing, Jessie. Mr. Cooke got so angry when we wouldn't show him the things we found out at Howling Cliffs. Maybe he was the one in the alleyway yesterday, trying to see if we had anything valuable. I wonder if he had something to do with the robbery."

Jessie rushed ahead of everyone. "I didn't want to mention him in front of the police officer in case I'm wrong. Let's just stop by his shop and take a look around."

The children stopped when they got to the shop.

"Well, who's going in there first?" Benny asked nervously.

"I'll go in first," Violet said, to her brothers' and sister's surprise. "I like the pretty things in his shop. If I'm nice to him, maybe he'll be nice to me."

"That's the way to go, Violet," Henry

said, proud of his sister. "Mr. Cooke can't help being nice to you."

Violet stepped inside the tiny shop. Every space was crammed with bone and tooth carvings from the great whaling days of Ragged Cove.

"What is it, miss?" Mr. Cooke asked when he saw Violet standing there.

Violet pointed to a small piece of scrimshaw in a glass case. "I'd like to look at that pie crimper for our housekeeper, Mrs. McGregor."

The man took another look at this bright little girl. "How did you know this was a pie crimper? Most folks don't have any idea of how it's used. Half of 'em think it's some kind of toy. You seem to know something about old things."

Violet smiled her sweet smile. "I use a wooden one like it when I bake with Mrs. McGregor. Ours isn't nearly as pretty as this one with the little unicorn decoration. How much is it?"

"Two hundred dollars, I'm afraid," Mr. Cooke said. "It's very unusual, one of my

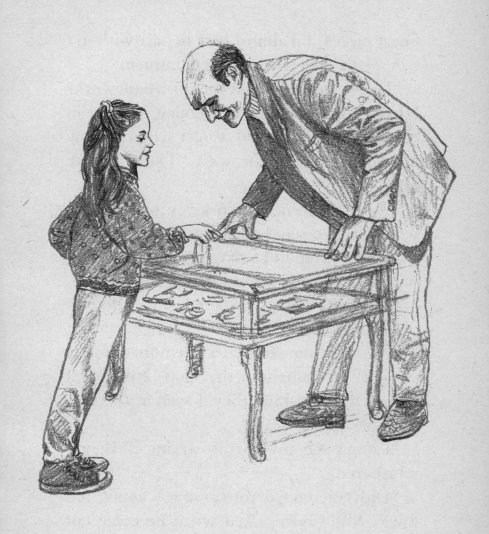

finest pieces. I'd almost hate to part with it."

Violet's face fell in disappointment.

"Does your housekeeper do needlework? I have some antique whalebone needles in back," Mr. Cooke told Violet when he saw how disappointed she was. "They're quite reasonable."

"We both do needlework," Violet said. "I would like to see the needles."

Violet waved in Henry, Jessie, and Benny when Mr. Cooke went into the back room. "He's nice," she whispered. "He doesn't seem a bit like a thief."

The children tried to memorize every piece of scrimshaw in the shop. None of it looked like anything they'd seen at the museum.

"I don't see any parrot carvings," Benny whispered.

"Did you say parrot carvings, young fellow?" Mr. Cooke asked when he came out front. "Sorry, the only one I've ever seen is carved on a whale tooth right in our excellent museum."

Benny stepped up to the counter. "Well,

we've seen it, too. Yesterday, we found another one in that postbox. Only it was carved on a small, flat piece. And guess what? It was the same parrot Miss Coffin had when she was small like me! We gave it to her for the museum."

"Well, you are a remarkable boy," Mr. Cooke said. "I'm going to give you a small reward for giving what you found to the museum."

"You are?" Benny said. "Heck, it was easy. All I did was climb this ledge. It was pretty high. Higher than this shop almost, and there it was. This old box with all these old things in it. The parrot picture, some bent-up old spoons, and some whale toys."

"Whale toys?" Mr. Cooke said. "Well, I have some whale toys. Here's an antique top. What do you think of that?"

Benny gave the top a spin on the counter. "I think I like it better than the parrot tooth."

Mr. Cooke handed Violet a small painted Chinese box. "And for your sister here, I have something special. Go ahead, open it, young lady."

Violet opened the box. Lying inside on a piece of satin was a matched set of bone needles from tiny to big. "Oooh," Violet breathed. "They're beautiful. I'll put them right into my sewing bag when I get back to the inn. Thank you."

"And thank you children for bringing your things to our Sailors' Museum," Mr. Cooke said to everyone. "I'm on the board there. We haven't many funds to buy things. So it helps when we get donations. I especially would like to see the parrot carving you found in the box."

"Why?" Benny wanted to know.

Mr. Cooke smiled. "Because I knew that parrot when I was a boy! Miss Coffin and I were best friends. Both our families used to spend the summer out on Plum Island where I live now. Prudence moved to town a few years ago when the ferry service slowed down. She hardly ever leaves the museum anymore unless I motor her out to the island on her boat. Myself, I'm a rowing man. Well, I'll go over and talk to her about your find."

Jessie stared at Mr. Cooke. "You mean you

didn't hear about Miss Coffin? She reported that there was a robbery at the museum last night, but now no one can find her."

Mr. Cooke held onto the counter. His pink face grew pale. "Prudence is gone?"

Mr. Cooke pulled down a sailor's pea coat from a hook by the front door. Underneath was a blue wool sailor cap just like Benny's. The children stared at the hat.

"I'll have to go look for her," Mr. Cooke said. "This is terrible. She never leaves that museum. Something must be very wrong. You'll have to leave. I'm going to close up and look for her."

Mr. Cooke put up his "Closed" sign and locked the door to his shop. The children watched him go down the narrow street away from town.

"Why is he heading toward the beach?" Jessie wondered.

By the time the children followed Mr. Cooke, he was gone, and so was his little rowboat.

CHAPTER 9

A Whale of a Time

At lunch the guests at the Black Dog Inn could talk of nothing but the museum robbery.

"If you ask me," one guest said, "the police should question Miss Coffin first. After all, she lives at the Sailors' Museum."

"Humph!" another guest said. "What about investigating the biggest scrimshaw dealer in these parts, Spooner Cooke? He's another strange one, always in that rowboat of his at odd hours."

This last comment about Spooner Cooke

upset Violet. She put down her soup spoon and spoke up. "Mr. Cooke only rows his boat at different times because of the tides and weather. We visited him just a little while ago. He was as nice as could be."

"Nice to children?" one person asked with raised eyebrows. "As long as we've been coming to Ragged Cove he hasn't let a child so much as look in the window of his shop."

Benny reached into his pocket, pulled out his scrimshaw top, and whirled it next to his clam chowder bowl. "Well, today he gave me this as a present. And he gave Violet a whole bunch of needles. All kinds."

Mrs. Pease came around with the soup pot. "There are different sides to everyone," she said. "Now, who wants seconds on chowder?"

For once Benny didn't want seconds. "I'm saving room for apple pie," he said, giving Mrs. Pease a big smile.

"Well, you'd better start your pie now," Mr. Pease said when he overheard this. "I just found out Captain Hull is setting out on a whale watch with a bus group that came down from Bassville. I asked him for a few more tickets for some of our guests. So whoever wants can have a whale of a good time."

"Let's go find some whales!" Mr. Alden told his grandchildren.

When the Aldens arrived at the docks, a tour group was boarding the *Jonah*. The children and their grandfather stood at the end of the line with tickets in hand. The line moved slowly up the gangplank.

Mr. Alden handed Captain Bob their five tickets. "Hi there, captain. I finally finished my business, so I can go out and see some of those whales my grandchildren told me about."

Captain Bob stared at the Aldens. "Uh . . . gee, Mr. Alden, where did you get these tickets?"

Mr. Alden took a closer look at the tickets. "Why, from you, of course. Mr. Pease said you gave him some for the Black Dog guests. That's us, you know. Is something wrong?"

The captain's face reddened. "It's just that I don't have any room today, sir. This tour group from Bassville pretty well fills the boat. I'll be going out in a couple days. I'll take you then."

Mr. Alden shook his head. "We have to be on our way tomorrow, so this is our last chance."

Several other tourists overheard Mr. Alden. A man stepped forward from his group to speak to Captain Bob. "Let these folks take our place. Our group has decided to come back tomorrow when it's sunnier."

"Then we can take their places, captain, wouldn't you say?" Mr. Alden asked.

A shadow seemed to pass over the captain's face. Finally, he took the Aldens' tickets and stuffed them into his pocket. "Life jackets are over there," was all he said before he rushed below deck.

The Aldens settled themselves on a bench at the front of the *Jonah*. "I can't imagine why Captain Bob didn't want our family on board," Mr. Alden said. "He seems out of sorts for some reason."

One of the passengers leaned on the railing near the Aldens and pointed toward Howling Cliffs. "Look. There are those lights again. Didn't I tell you, Millie, that I saw some lights over that way before the last storm?"

The children jumped up to see what the man was talking about. Sure enough, flickering lights shone over the water near Howling Cliffs.

The man went on. "Captain! Captain! Aren't those lights supposed to be from that wreck the uh . . . ."

"The *Flying Cloud*," Jessie finished. "Or the lights have something to do with the weather. They only come out when there are storm clouds."

"What's your opinion on that, Captain Bob?" the man asked. "You're the expert in these waters."

Captain Bob just piloted the *Jonah* straight ahead, as if there were nothing unusual at all about lights coming from nowhere.

"Leave him alone," the man's wife whispered. "He's looking out for whales, not ghosts."

Everyone nearby except for Captain Bob had a good laugh over this comment. Just as

Jessie had said, once the clouds disappeared, so did the strange lights.

"Whale off! Whale off!" Benny cried a while later. "Look, Captain Bob. There's a pod of whales."

All the passengers moved to the front of the boat. Everyone could see the shiny gray backs of at least six whales.

"Oh, look!" Violet cried with delight. "There's a baby whale on its mother's back! How wonderful!"

"It's a whale calf," Captain Bob said from behind the wheel of the *Jonah*. His voice seemed gentler now that there were whales nearby. "That's how the young ones ride around until they're old enough to leave their mothers. They stay safe that way. Whoa!" he yelled out suddenly. "Everybody sit down on the benches or go below deck! There's a big whale ready to breach right by us!"

Mr. Alden motioned for Henry, Violet, Jessie, and Benny to head below deck.

"What's 'breach' mean, Grandfather?" Benny asked, holding on to the rail of the narrow stairs.

"That's when a whale suddenly breaks to the surface," Mr. Alden explained. "That one came awfully close to this boat."

"My tummy feels funny," Benny said as the *Jonah* rocked back and forth.

"I bet that big whale made some big waves," Henry said. "That's why the boat is rocking like this."

Everyone tried to hold on to each other when the *Jonah* made a sharp turn. Some metal dishes slid and crashed to the floor. Several cans of food rolled around. Cabinet doors opened. Out fell books, ropes, boxes, and tools. The boat pitched back and forth for several long minutes before it settled down.

"Let's put away some of these things that fell out," Jessie said.

Mr. Alden and the older children started to pick up all the objects that had fallen to the floor. They returned everything to its proper place. Then Jessie noticed something way under the table.

"Look at this," Jessie whispered to Henry. She held up a black, leather-covered book

that said: *Diary: Captain Coffin* on the front.

The Aldens heard the *Jonah*'s engines stop. They looked up and saw Captain Bob's black rubber boots on the stairs.

"Everybody and everything okay down here?" Captain Bob yelled down below. "Hope nobody got seasick."

Jessie quickly replaced the diary in the cabinet.

"We're fine now that the boat's not rocking," Mr. Alden told Captain Bob when he came to see how the Aldens were doing. "But I think we'll head up for some fresh air."

The captain looked around. "Thanks for cleaning up. I forgot to lock up some of these cabinets. I'd better do that now in case another whale decides he wants to ride nearly piggyback with us."

The children watched Captain Bob go straight to the cabinet where the logbook was hidden. He put a small lock through it and snapped it shut.

"Everything's where it should be now," Captain Bob said. "Let's find some more whales."

CHAPTER 10

No More Secrets

Benny packed his flashlight in his suitcase the next morning. "I guess I don't need it anymore on this trip," he said. "We had two adventures: the big storm and finding that old postbox."

"Don't forget about seeing all those whales," Henry said.

Benny tossed his clothes into his suitcase. "Whales are fun, not an adventure. I wish we'd seen that ghost ship."

"And I'm glad we didn't," Violet said, carefully tucking a small bag of beach glass and shells into her tote bag. "I only wish we had time to look for Miss Coffin and say good-bye to her."

Mr. Pease overheard Violet when he came up to the Crow's Nest to give the children a message. "If you want to see about Miss Coffin, you do have time. Your grandfather is delayed. There are quite a few other people who would like to see Prudence too. The police can't seem to crack the museum robbery without her."

"Then let's go look for her," Jessie suggested. "I'd like to find out what happened at the museum."

"Good luck to you," Mr. Pease said.

The Aldens stopped at the beach to take one last look at the ocean.

"Look, I think that's Spooner Cooke rowing in," Violet said. "He's going to be late opening his shop."

The children jumped up and down and waved at the small boat out on the water, but the boater didn't wave back.

" 'Bye, Ragged Cove," Violet said, still waving. "I'm going to make a beach in a jar when we get home with some of the sand and shells I collected."

The children left the beach and headed into town. Out of habit, they stopped to look in the shop windows.

"Let's go by Mr. Cooke's shop later on our way back from the museum," Violet said. "I want to thank him again and say good-bye. I wish he were at his shop already."

Jessie grabbed Violet's arm. "He is!" she cried. "Look, there's a light on."

Henry cupped his hands over the window to get a better look. "That can't be Mr. Cooke. We just saw him in his boat. It must be somebody else. Whoever it is just went upstairs."

Violet knocked and turned the doorknob. "It's us, Mr. Cooke. We came to say good-bye," she yelled through the glass door.

There was no answer, just a light that suddenly went out in the shop.

"Maybe he hires somebody to clean the shop and they don't want to bother with customers so early," Henry said. "We can try later."

When the Aldens reached the Sailors' Museum it was locked tight. A yellow plastic banner across the door said: *Crime Scene. Off Limits*.

Violet shivered. "Poor Miss Coffin. She must still be missing."

Henry led his brother and sisters away from the museum. "We have to talk to Spooner Cooke. He's her oldest friend. Maybe he has some idea where she might be. He said he was going to look for her."

"What about Captain Bob?" Benny asked. "He's the only one besides us who saw what was in the postbox. He acted funny when we said we wanted to bring it to Miss Coffin for the museum. What about him, Henry?"

Jessie spoke up before Henry could answer. "Now, now. We mustn't get too many ideas yet, Benny. After all, Captain Bob and Mr. Cooke and even Miss Coffin have been nice to us — not at all like people who would steal things or hurt anyone."

Violet looked upset. "But . . . but, Jessie. What about the old diary that fell out of Captain Bob's cabinet on the *Jonah*? I don't want to think that someone who loves whales so much could be hiding something, but he was."

Henry took Benny and Violet by the hand. " 'First things first,' Grandfather always says. Let's see about Spooner Cooke, then we can look for Captain Bob."

Mr. Cooke's shop was still closed when the Aldens arrived.

"That's funny," Jessie began. "We saw Mr. Cooke coming into shore in his boat. He should be here by now."

Jessie went up to the window and looked inside. The store was dark again. "Whoever was in there before must be gone. I don't see anyone inside now."

While the older children were talking, Benny went around to the side of the building. "Hey, wait a minute. There *is* somebody in there now, Jessie! *Two* somebodies just came down the stairs."

"It's Mr. Cooke and Miss Coffin!" Henry said when he saw what Benny saw. "They just went into the storage room behind the shop."

"Mr. Cooke! Miss Coffin!" Jessie shouted as she rapped on the back door. "It's the Aldens."

Slowly, the back door opened. The children stepped inside. Sitting at a cluttered work table was Miss Coffin. And spread out in front of her was the postbox along with the scrimshaw and a pile of old papers and books.

"Miss Coffin!" Jessie cried. "I'm so glad you're all right."

But Miss Coffin wasn't all right. She looked frightened and upset.

"Why are you here?" Violet asked in a gentle voice. "We were worried about you."

Miss Coffin tried to speak, but no words came out.

"That's okay, Miss Coffin," Jessie said before turning to Spooner Cooke. "Can you tell us what happened, Mr. Cooke?"

Mr. Cooke didn't speak right away. He just pointed to a book that said: *Logbook: The Flying Cloud.* Jessie recognized the old leather book that had been in the barrel. "Read the entries on the last page," he whispered in a shaky voice. "Then you'll know why Prudence took these things away from the museum."

Jessie began reading:

"November 4, 1869: Captain Coffin sick for ten days with malaria. Ordered crew to go back to open sea.

"November 5, 1869: Captain's condition very grave. Crew met to discuss situation. Supplies low. Captain wandered on deck, confused by fever. Again ordered crew to return to sea. Decision made to lock him in cabin for safety. Crew appointed first mate, Eli Hull, as new leader until Captain Coffin recovers. Captain kept screaming: 'Mutiny! Mutiny!' All medical supplies gone. Decision made to head for Ragged Cove. Captain feverish and crying over and over: 'Emily! Emily!' Storm clouds blowing from northeast.

"November 6, 1869: Captain Coffin died at 10:00 P.M. last night. Will send cabin boy to put papers in coast postbox before storm hits."

"That's all there is?" Violet asked in a whisper.

Mr. Cooke took the logbook from Jessie.

"November sixth is the day the *Flying Cloud* burned and sank. This was a terrible shock for Prudence. Now you know why she wanted to keep this logbook hidden from the public."

Spooner Cooke sat by his old friend and took her hand. "There, there, Prudence. I told you that what your great-grandfather did is no disgrace. Malaria is one of the worst sicknesses a sailor fears. It clouds the mind."

"That's what Gabby the parrot said — 'capsick, capsick'!" Benny cried.

"Yes, I suppose you're right." Miss Coffin looked up and spoke in a faraway voice. "He *was* a hero, I know he was. That's what my grandparents and parents always told me. That's what I put in my book. But I was wrong."

Spooner Cooke tried to comfort Miss Coffin. "It's not wrong if you don't know all the facts. Your great-grandfather was heading to safety when sickness took over his mind. There's nothing shameful about that."

Miss Coffin looked around the small room at everyone standing there. "But there is something shameful about hiding this log-book, Spooner. I took the scrimshaw pieces so everyone would think there had been a robbery and that everything inside the cannon barrel was stolen too. I have disgraced our wonderful family name after all. And I even involved you by coming here, Spooner. I should have stayed out on Plum Island where I had taken everything in my old motorboat."

"Now, now Prudence," Mr. Cooke said. "You're safe and sound here, and so are all the missing things now that we got them back from Plum Island."

"Not all the missing . . ." Benny started to say.

Jessie took Benny's hand before he finished his sentence. "I just remembered there's something we have to do," she said. "Thank you for showing that to us. We'll leave you two alone now."

"Whew, Benny," Henry said when everyone was outside. "You got us out of there just in time, Jessie."

Benny looked up at his older brother. "Just

in time for what, Henry?"

"Just in time to keep you from telling Miss Coffin that Captain Bob might have her great-grandfather's diary," Jessie explained.

"Yes, we don't want to upset her even more until we find out about it," Violet added. "Poor Miss Coffin."

The children were halfway down the street when they heard a voice behind them.

"Benny! Aldens! Wait!" The voice belonged to Captain Bob. "You left your horseshoe crab shell on the *Jonah*, Benny. Here it is." The captain handed the shell to him. "Hey, what's the matter? I thought you'd be glad to get this."

Benny stared down at his sneakers. "You can keep it."

The captain looked at the Aldens. "All of you seem upset. Is something wrong?"

Jessie couldn't bring herself to look at Captain Bob. "Maybe you should go to Mr. Cooke's shop. Miss Coffin is there too."

Captain Bob seemed confused. "As a matter of fact that's just where I was going. I

wanted to show Spooner the old diary I found in the cannon barrel. I figured he could take it to the museum when Miss Coffin gets back. I knew she wouldn't want to see me," he said in a sad voice.

"So that diary was in the cannon barrel!" Henry said. "We spotted it when it fell out of a cabinet on your boat. Why did you hide it?"

Captain Bob pulled out the old leather diary from the other shoebox. "When you read this, you'll find out. It's Captain Coffin's diary. It was the only thing I had time to look at the day I opened the cannon barrel down in my boat. I tried to find out what else was in the cannon barrel after you children took everything to the museum, but I decided not to."

"We thought somebody came in," Henry said. "We heard the door bang."

"I changed my mind," Captain Bob said. "I couldn't take something that rightfully belonged to the museum. That's why I want to return this diary to its proper place. You'll know everything about the *Flying Cloud* when you read what's in it."

When the captain and the Aldens got to the shop, Miss Coffin was closing up a box she had packed with the missing items. Her whole face darkened when she saw the children with Captain Bob.

"I have something else to put in that box." Captain Bob handed Miss Coffin the diary.

"What is this?" Miss Coffin asked.

"Your great-grandfather's diary. I guess you were right. My great-great grandfather, Eli Hull, did try to take over the *Flying Cloud* from Captain Coffin just as you said in your book. That's what your great-grandfather wrote in here anyway."

"Now, now, young man," Miss Coffin said in a steady voice. "Eli Hull did take over the *Flying Cloud*, but only because my great-grandfather was not in his right mind owing to a terrible sickness. He probably wrote the diary when his mind was confused by his illness. The last account of the *Flying Cloud* is in this logbook. It proves your great-great grandfather, Eli Hull, was the real hero."

Captain Bob took the logbook and read the

last page. His voice was quiet when he finally spoke up. "All these years I've been looking for something like this. After every storm I would go up and down the coast near where the *Flying Cloud* went down. I just had to know that my great-great grandfather didn't start a mutiny. When I saw the diary in the cannon barrel, I hid it away without looking at the other things in there."

Miss Coffin stood up. "Well, that just goes to show that you and I don't make very good thieves, do we now?"

"That's for sure," Benny said. "If Captain Bob had had the logbook, and Miss Coffin the diary, then everybody would've been happy."

They all smiled at this.

"Well, everybody is happy now," Spooner Cooke said.

"Not quite," Miss Coffin said. "Don't forget, my book is all wrong now. Why, everybody will be talking about nothing else but that!"

Benny went up to Miss Coffin. "Not if you write a new book."

Miss Coffin gave Benny a friendly tap on his nose. "And I know just what I'll call my new book."

Benny wanted to hear the title. "What?"

"Benny: The Boy Who Couldn't Stop Talking."

"I'll want to read that when we come back to Ragged Cove someday," Jessie said, laughing with everyone.

Benny had one more thing to talk about. "We have to come back to find out about those lights we saw and those voices we heard at Howling Cliffs. Did anybody find anything about that in these old books and papers?"

Captain Hull and Miss Coffin both shook their heads.

"Not a thing," Spooner Cooke said. "That will always be a mystery."

"Goody," Benny said. "Now I'm sure we'll be back!"

GERTRUDE CHANDLER WARNER discovered when she was teaching that many readers who like an exciting story could find no books that were both easy and fun to read. She decided to try to meet this need, and her first book, *The Boxcar Children*, quickly proved she had succeeded.

Miss Warner drew on her own experiences to write each mystery. As a child she spent hours watching trains go by on the tracks opposite her family home. She often dreamed about what it would be like to set up housekeeping in a caboose or freight car — the situation the Alden children find themselves in.

When Miss Warner received requests for more adventures involving Henry, Jessie, Violet, and Benny Alden, she began additional stories. In each, she chose a special setting and introduced unusual or eccentric characters who liked the unpredictable.

While the mystery element is central to each of Miss Warner's books, she never thought of them as strictly juvenile mysteries. She liked to stress the Aldens' independence and resourcefulness and their solid New England devotion to using up and making do. The Aldens go about most of their adventures with as little adult supervision as possible — something else that delights young readers.

Miss Warner lived in Putnam, Connecticut, until her death in 1979. During her lifetime, she received hundreds of letters from girls and boys telling her how much they liked her books.